The Smart Mouse

by Regina Velázquez
illustrated by Mircea Catusanu

HOUGHTON MIFFLIN

BOSTON

Printed in India

ISBN-13: 978-0-547-02552-0
ISBN-10: 0-547-02552-1

2 3 4 5 6 7 8 9 0940 15 14 13 12 11 10

Mouse lived by the river. He was very smart. He had a nice home. He had lots of food to eat. He was very happy. He did not want or need anything else.

Mouse

Then one day Mouse looked across the river. He saw trees full of tasty fruit. The trees were beside the village on the other side of the river. Now Mouse wanted the fruit on the opposite riverbank. He leaned over the river to look at the fruit more closely.

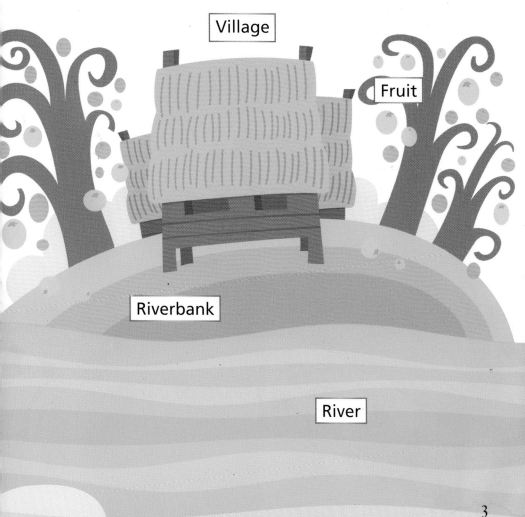

Village

Fruit

Riverbank

River

Suddenly, Crocodile jumped from the river. Crocodile tried to bite Mouse. Mouse was startled, or scared. He jumped back.

So Mouse had a problem. Mouse wanted the fruit across the river. But Mouse knew he could not get into the river. Crocodile would eat up poor Mouse!

Crocodile

Mouse thought, "How can I get that fruit? Crocodile lives in the river. I know I am smarter than Crocodile. I must think of a good plan."

Mouse began to search for another way across the river. He could not see any other way. Mouse thought and thought. Finally, he thought of the perfect plan!

The next day, Mouse went down to the river. He said loudly, "Crocodile!"

Crocodile thought it was odd for Mouse to call him. But Crocodile stuck his head out of the river anyway.

"What do you want, Mouse?" asked Crocodile. "Do you want to be my breakfast?"

Mouse answered, "No. I have important news from the King to share."

"The King!" said Crocodile. "What is the news?"

"The King is having a big fancy meal. He wants to invite the crocodiles. I have to count all the crocodiles in the river. Then the King will know how much food to serve," said Mouse.

Sharing news

Crocodile came out of the river. "How can I help?" he asked Mouse.

"Please ask all the crocodiles to make a line. The crocodiles should line up from this side of the river to the other. Then I can count all the crocodiles," said Mouse.

The river contained many crocodiles. Crocodile dove into the river. He told his family and friends what to do. The crocodiles tossed and turned in the river. They all lined up from head to tail. The crocodiles made a line from one side of the river to the other.

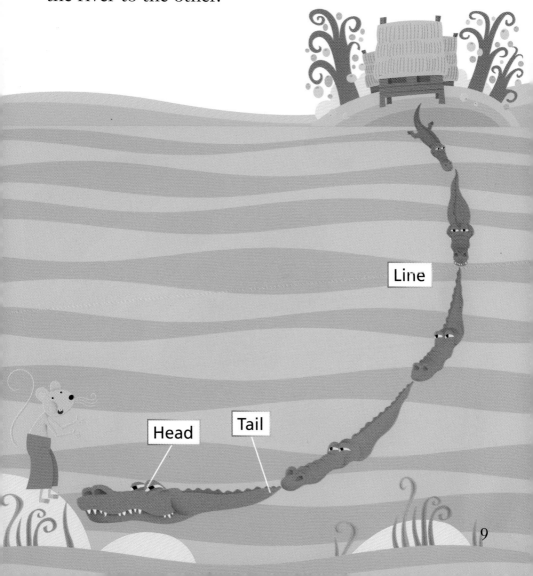

Line

Head

Tail

"The line is perfect! Thank you. I'm grateful for your help," Mouse said to the crocodiles. "Now before I count you, please promise me one thing."

"What is that?" the crocodiles asked.

"Please do not eat me while I am counting. I have to report to the King," Mouse said. "There will be no feast for you if I cannot report to the King."

"We will not eat you," promised the crocodiles. They thought only of the King's feast.

Feast

11

Mouse jumped on top of Crocodile's head. Mouse counted, "One." He jumped on another crocodile's head and said, "Two." He jumped and counted again and again. At last, he reached the other side of the river. He was very close to the tasty fruit.

Fruit

Crocodile asked Mouse, "How many crocodiles are there? What will you report to the King?"

Mouse smiled. He said, "There are just enough crocodiles to get me across the river. I will tell the King that Mouse is smarter than Crocodile any day!"

Mouse ran off to eat the fruit in the trees beside the village. The crocodiles were mad. But they knew that Mouse had played a smart trick on them.

Eating

Responding

✔ TARGET SKILL **Understanding Characters** Think about the characters of Mouse and Crocodile in the story. Copy and complete the chart below.

Character	Action	What It Means
Mouse	He tells Crocodile there will be a feast.	Mouse knows what Crocodile wants.
?	?	?

Write About It

Text to Text Think about another story in which a character plays a trick. Is it right to trick someone? Write a paragraph about the trick. Give your opinion. Include examples that tell more about your opinion.

✔ **TARGET SKILL** **Understanding Characters** Tell more about the characters.

✔ **TARGET STRATEGY** **Summarize** Stop to tell important events as you read.

GENRE A **folktale** is a story that is often told by people of a country.